For Katharina and my tiger

Copyright © 2019 by NordSüd Verlag AG, CH8050 Zürich, Switzerland.
First published in Switzerland under the title *Willys Wunderwelt*.
English text copyright © 2019 by NorthSouth Books Inc., New York 10016.
Translated by David Henry Wilson.
Design and typesetting by Silvia Wahrstätter / vielseitig.co.at, Willy Puchner.

First published in the United States, Great Britain, Canada, Australia, and New
Zealand in 2019 by NorthSouth Books, Inc., an imprint of NordSüd Verlag AG,
CH-8050 Zürich, Switzerland.

Distributed in the United States by NorthSouth Books Inc., New York 10016.
Library of Congress Cataloging-in-Publication Data is available.
ISBN: 978-0-7358-4383-7
Printed in Latvia by Livonia Print, Riga, 2018.
1 3 5 7 9 • 10 8 6 4 2
www.northsouth.com

Willy Puchner
Willy's World of Wonders

North
South

Willy's World of Wonders

Life is a wonder, a miracle, and a mystery.
When I use my imagination, I can travel into worlds that give me pleasure
and hope or cheer me up if I'm feeling sad. I can stand astonished,
sit and dream, or escape from the daily grind.
In my imagination I can fly through the clouds on a bird,
hover across the sky in my balloon, perform in a circus,
or climb into a boat and sail the seven seas. So off I go, smelling the air
and wandering into a different world—my world of wonders.
Sometimes there are things that bring back memories,
maybe evoking images from my childhood. The present links up with the past.
I can experience them both through my writing and my drawing,
and I can enrich them by making them into something magical and fantastic.
What I like best of all is to revel
in a mixture of astonishment and enchantment.
Would you like to join me?

World of Color

Fond and foolish I may be, but I'm happy
as a man can be. I shine like a peacock, look superb,
and am all dressed up in my richest robes.
I feel full of life, on top of the world,
in the best of spirits, and as bright as the sun.
Animals make me feel happy,
with all their bright colors.

How to Do a Doodle

If you want to enter the world of wonders,
you'll need all kinds of materials and instruments:
drawing paper, different sized cards, pads full of
blank pages, soft pencils, hard pencils, colored
pencils, a pencil sharpener, an eraser, paints and
paintbrushes, a palette, bowls of water, pieces of
cloth, fountain pens, old stamps, new stamps,
a homemade rubber stamp, glue, a magnifying glass
objects you find in nature, sunshine,
and all the joys of a rainbow.

Willy's World of Wonders

AIRMAIL

Fantasia 1.00

Ocean

For many years I've had my own little circus ring,
where all kinds of people do all kinds of things. They enter
the ring, perform under the lights, and then disappear.
My circus accompanies me ... always and everywhere.

I was once an acrobat in a flea circus.
I pulled a merry-go-round and raced
against other fleas. I was lucky enough
to escape, and now I'm looking for
another host.

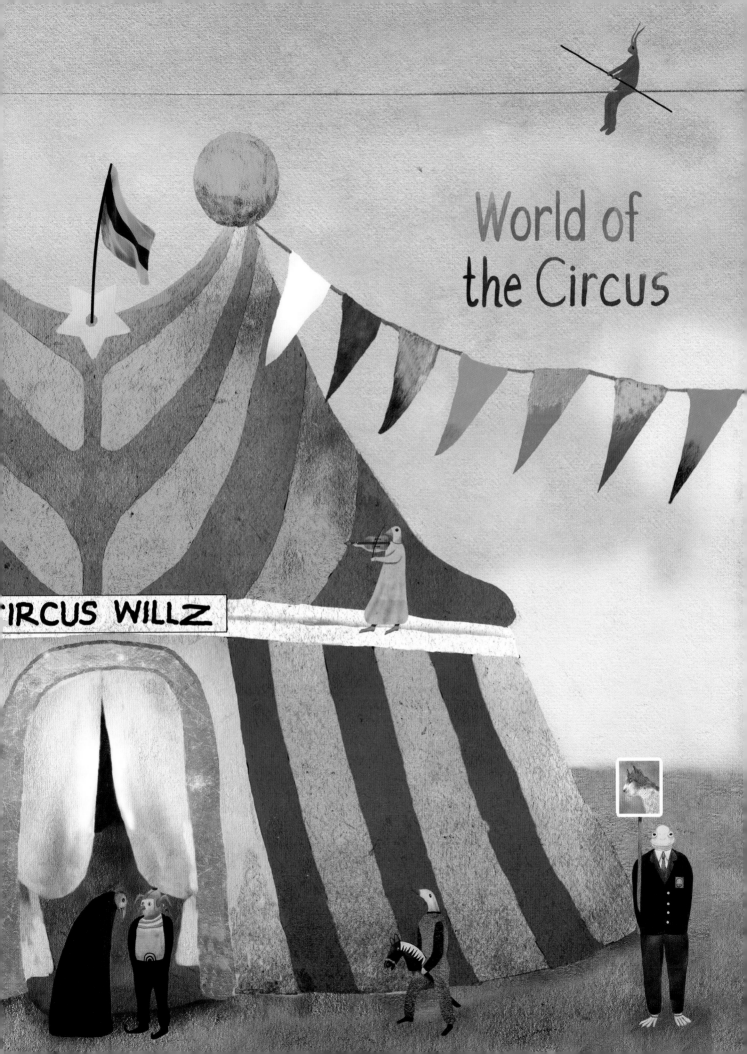

World of the Circus

CIRCUS WILLZ

When I lie down under my warm blanket,
I travel out into the wide world. I hoist the sails,
and my bed becomes a boat, and my room becomes
the open sea. The waves splash beneath me,
gently rocking me to and fro, and I feel a soft breeze
wafting over me. Clouds as white and soft as sheep
drift across the sky. At once I am filled with excitement
and joy. Suddenly a dragon-like sea monster
bursts out of the water and whispers to me:
"If you can tell me how many heads I have,
I'll let you go on dreaming."

World of Dreams

Underwater World

The inhabitants of the miniature ocean
live in perfect peace. The aquarium is an El Dorado,
a place of beauty, lazy slow motion, and great pleasure.
Lola and Linus swim in the center,
caressing each other all day long, while their family
of triplets—Koko, Kiki, and Kuki—watch with interes
Admiral Anton glides contentedly from left to right
and back again, Honey hides under the seagrass,
and Red Lady seems to have had an idea.
But will she share it with the others?

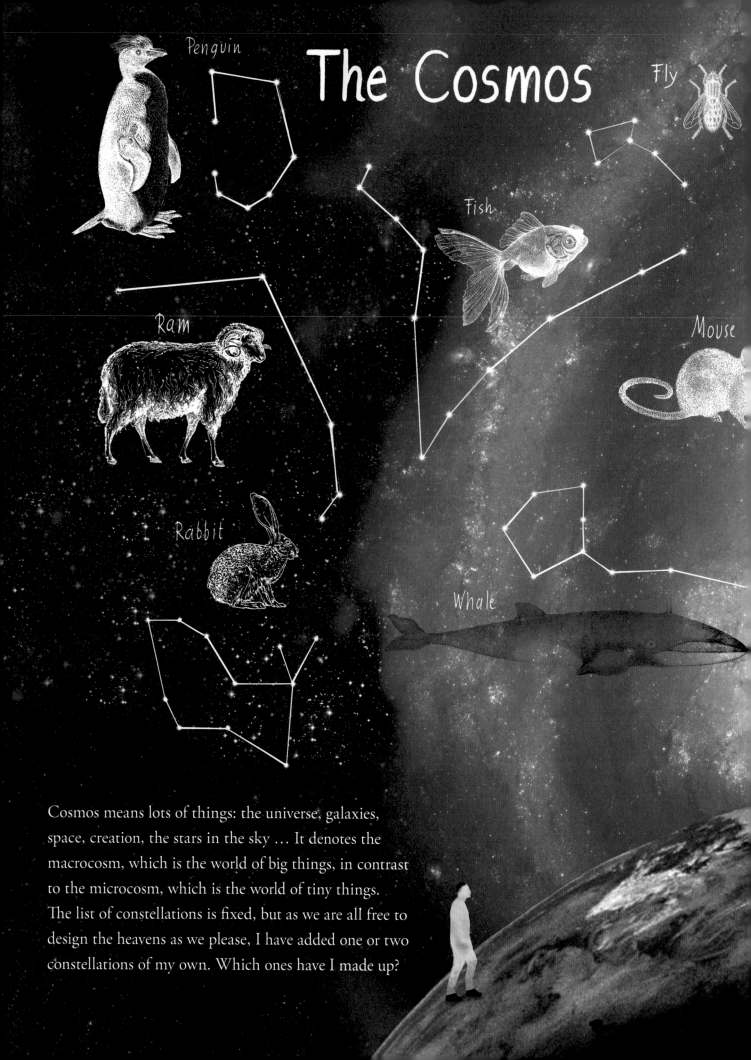

The Cosmos

Penguin

Fly

Fish

Mouse

Ram

Rabbit

Whale

Cosmos means lots of things: the universe, galaxies,
space, creation, the stars in the sky … It denotes the
macrocosm, which is the world of big things, in contrast
to the microcosm, which is the world of tiny things.
The list of constellations is fixed, but as we are all free to
design the heavens as we please, I have added one or two
constellations of my own. Which ones have I made up?

On my travels I often fly
in my balloon.
Generally, it's a seagull balloon
that glides silently up into the sky
or down into the depths.
I'm not in the least afraid. Why should I be?
These trips are only made
in my imagination.

Above the Clouds

September 19, 1783:
The palace of Versailles was the first
launching site of a Montgolfiere,
and it had three passengers:
a duck, a chicken and a ram.
King Louis XVI. and Marie Antoinette
were watching. There was, however,
an unfortunate accident:
the ram stepped on the chicken.

00:0

Time Trave

0:01

I'm a time traveler. I keep traveling back into the
past, remembering earlier periods of my life—
revisiting countries I've already seen, dreaming
of other eras, going back through history and
imagining all kinds of events. Then I move on
into the future and imagine what the world
might look like ten, a hundred, or a thousand
years from now. I wish I had a time machine
that would really take me out of the present.

19:17   18:48   22:22

World of
the Past

We're told that everything was different
in olden times. Women wore long dresses,
men liked wearing hats, and you can be sure
that they all thought very differently from us.
We're told that everything was slower,
cozier, and quieter. If only we could imagine
what it was really like …

World of Language

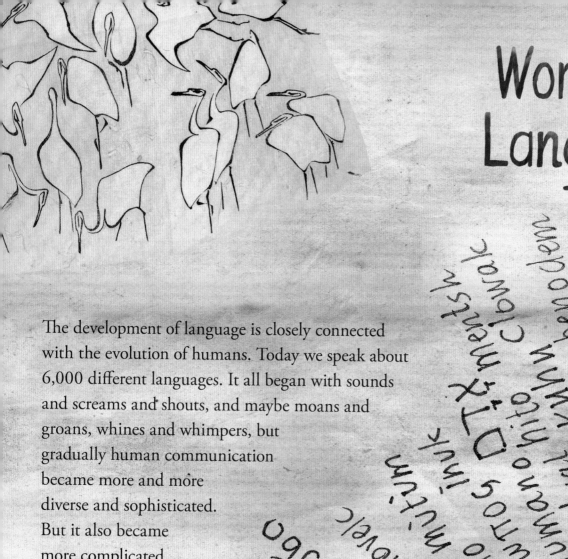

The development of language is closely connected with the evolution of humans. Today we speak about 6,000 different languages. It all began with sounds and screams and shouts, and maybe moans and groans, whines and whimpers, but gradually human communication became more and more diverse and sophisticated. But it also became more complicated, and therefore more difficult.

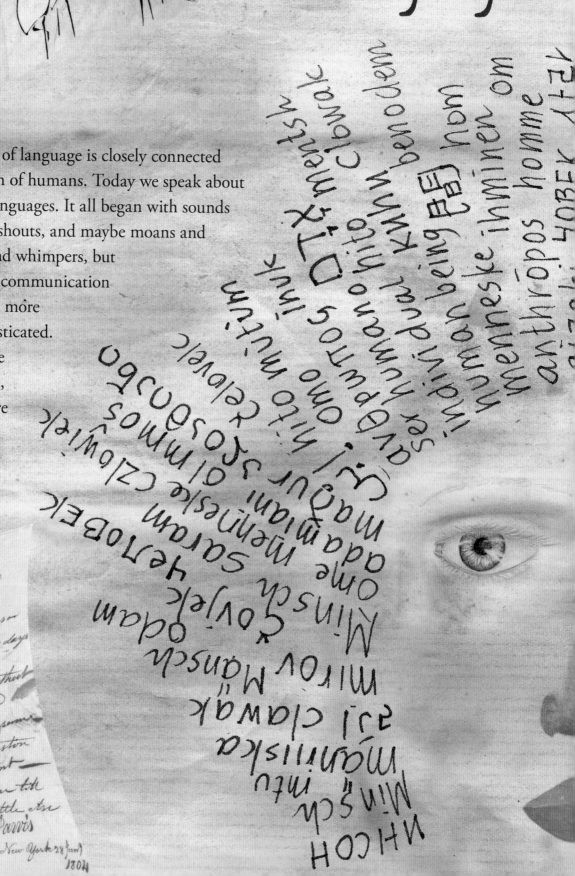

j.Mirov

insan
kewe den
čovēk homo ādām
human benkilo
menniskja hi homem
hingen persona
manusia
ésserhumà
individuo orang
uomo inuit homo
manneslkja člověk
manusya hombre
Mensch
cilvēks mtu nhãn
insan menš
nguròi persona
ember

World of Fantasy

Z

N

A

C

J

K

B

In the world of the imagination, anything and everything
is possible. You can have whatever you like whenever you
want it. Sometimes I travel on the back of a golden beetle,
or I fly across the world in a yellow airship.
Letters whirl through the air and I catch them,
make them into words, then sentences,
and finally a story.

V

F

Y

M

honeybee (Apis mellifera)

dragonfly (Libellula fluviatilis)

Bees whisper to one another
where to find the best nectar.
The dragonfly stretches out to extend his abdomen.
The centipede carries a sunshade.
The beetle covers himself with a leaf.
The spider sleeps in a green summer bed.
The grasshopper likes to sail through the world on a leaf.
The mayfly rehearses for her next appearance
when the new day dawns.

centipede (Myriapoda)

World of Little Wonders

mayfly (Ephemeroptera)

green cricket (Tettigonia viridissima)

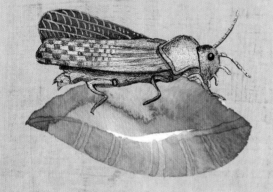

poplar leaf beetle (Chrysomela populi)

domestic spider (Tegenaria domestica)

Willyosaurus

Unimaginably impressive, but also rather scary, these giant lizards lived in prehistoric times, long before humans even existed. They were four or five times the size of us humans, and the wingspan of the pterodactyl was so big that you could have put a row of tiny houses on it.

Tyrannosaurus rex

World of Large Wonders

Quetzalcoatlus

Apatosaurus

Ankylosaurus

Best wishes on your birthday, dear little bird
with your red beak! Just born, and already
we're eager to see you and to hold you gently
in our hands. Oh, you're so small! So sweet!
How wonderful it is that you're here!

Bird Weddi

Caruso

Mucki

Lucky

H

Sunny

Spiri

Figaro

Zotto

Kitly

Queen

Sugar

The wedding was one big party. On the table was a feast of sunflower seeds, poppy and hemp seed gâteau, fish pie with snail sauce garnished with wild herbs, hazelnuts, fruit pips, cereals in a birdbath, and to top it all off, nectar juice and insect cake with raisins.

I love presents more than anything else.
Most of all I like it when the present is a surprise.
For instance, when people come to visit me and sing me a song or tell me a story,
or give me a sunshade, or a box and I can't guess what's hidden inside;
a mouth-watering soup, a letter, or something that arouses my curiosity.
Or quite simply, flowers.
I've often thought about this:
one day I sit on a throne, and the next I stand in a line.
It's not easy to be given the right present,
but it's even more difficult to give the right one.

World of Little Presents

For us the family is sacred. We celebrate each occasion and take every opportunity to get together. Fortunately, everybody has a birthday once a year, and a Saints' Day also. We love Easter and Christmas, and we all go on holiday together. Long live the world of the family!

Heinrich

Ulrich

Clara

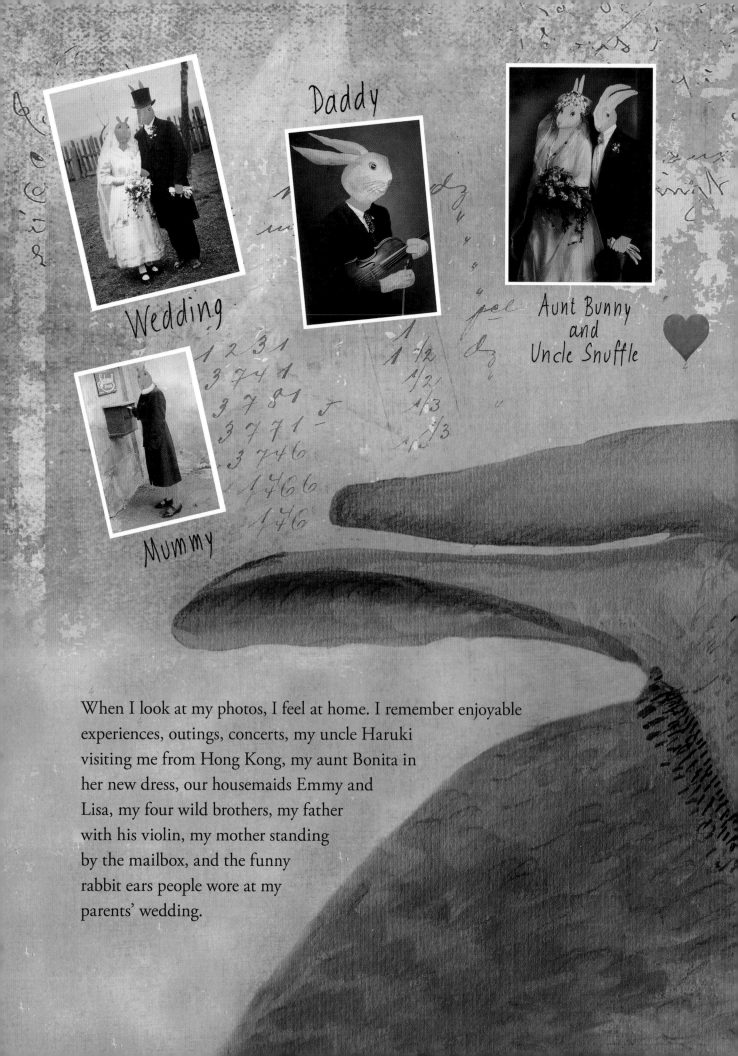

Daddy

Wedding

Aunt Bunny
and
Uncle Snuffle

Mummy

When I look at my photos, I feel at home. I remember enjoyable
experiences, outings, concerts, my uncle Haruki
visiting me from Hong Kong, my aunt Bonita in
her new dress, our housemaids Emmy and
Lisa, my four wild brothers, my father
with his violin, my mother standing
by the mailbox, and the funny
rabbit ears people wore at my
parents' wedding.

World of Photographs

Rocky, Bobby, Blotchy and Biggy

Uncle Haruki

Emmy
and Lisa

Aunt Bonita

Comforting Cats

When I'm sad, I look at cats, listen to them,
admire their elegance, watch their movements,
marvel at their beauty and their charm.
When I'm very sad, I dress them in a costume.
By changing them, just for a moment or two
I make them like me. And then, when I
begin to purr, I've conquered my sadness.

World of Fashion

Who has never dreamt of walking along a red carpet,
being gazed at and admired from all sides?
Maybe even greeted with thunderous applause! All the sam
I'm a bit uncertain whether people have realized that I'm
all dressed up in my new summer fur.

Catwalk

Procession

The announcement itself was sensational: *Tonight, the sun, moon, and stars will march along the ocean.* Lots of curious people wanted to watch the spectacle, and they were not disappointed. The procession lasted for a short time only, but it was beautiful and fascinating, and was accompanied by the ceaseless rise and fall of the ocean waves. I can't wait for the next procession of lights!

World of Rain

Rain! Rain! Rain!
It's like taking a shower in the open air—
a great waterfall that is there one moment
and gone the next: refreshing, sparkling, bountiful.
I stretch my arms up high, make myself bigger,
and rejoice with a cry of sheer joy.
At once a large, bright bird flies to me,
bringing me the seven colors of the rainbow.

World of Animals

I would love to slip into the skin of an animal.
I can imagine being all kinds of animals:
one day I'd be a monkey, the next a sheep,
and at Easter I'd be a bunny; and in the summer
I'd be a butterfly. If the weather was very hot,
I'd turn into a frog and dive into the water.
If I was a bird, I could fly, and if I was a cat,
I could purr.

TEAT

World of
Theater

BANALE

Jumping around is fun!
Jumping for joy. Jumping till you
run out of puff. And it's even better
if you can jump around with others,
leaping here and dancing there.
Keep jumping, and you'll feel your heart
jumping for joy as well.

My Paradise

There is a place we call paradise. But for each of us this place looks different. Also, the paradise of yesterday is not the same as the paradise of tomorrow. Paradise is a place for the moment. I once traveled with some friends to meet up with some other friends. It was then that all of us had a feeling of wonderful harmony and joy, which bound us together as if we were one. My friends are often my paradise.

Each letter is a small universe, a cosmos all on its own. In my world of letters, thoughts come rolling like balls—I tell stories, and often describe small incidents or big adventures. A letter globe is a piece of writing that spins in a circle. As the famous painter Vincent van Gogh once said: Life is round!

World of Letters

In my world of wonders, I wander off gazing at the sky. As I walk I sense the evenness of my steps, the rhythm I create on my journey into another world. I feel as if I am in a dream, a fairy land, and I would like to go where I have never been before—to be a bird flying with the flock, or a chicken that is as big as a continent. I long for different countries, to learn a foreign language, or to ride a camel across the desert. If you want to come with me, climb into my boat and together we'll sail into the great, big world.

OS
Wanderlust